DAWN OF A RUINOUS LOVE

DAWN OF A RUINOUS LOVE

A THAUMORIAN LEGENDS NOVELLA

THAUMORIAN LEGENDS

A M ENO

ISBN
979-8-9893390-4-4 (paperback)
979-8-9893390-5-1 (ebook)

ALSO BY A.M. ENO

THAUMORIAN LEGENDS

Novellas

Released

Origins of a Guild Master

Secrets of a Sagacious Witch

Dawn of a Ruinous Love

To Be Released

Creation of a Fated Thief

Heart of an Outcast Mistress

Novels

To Be Released

The Death Bringer

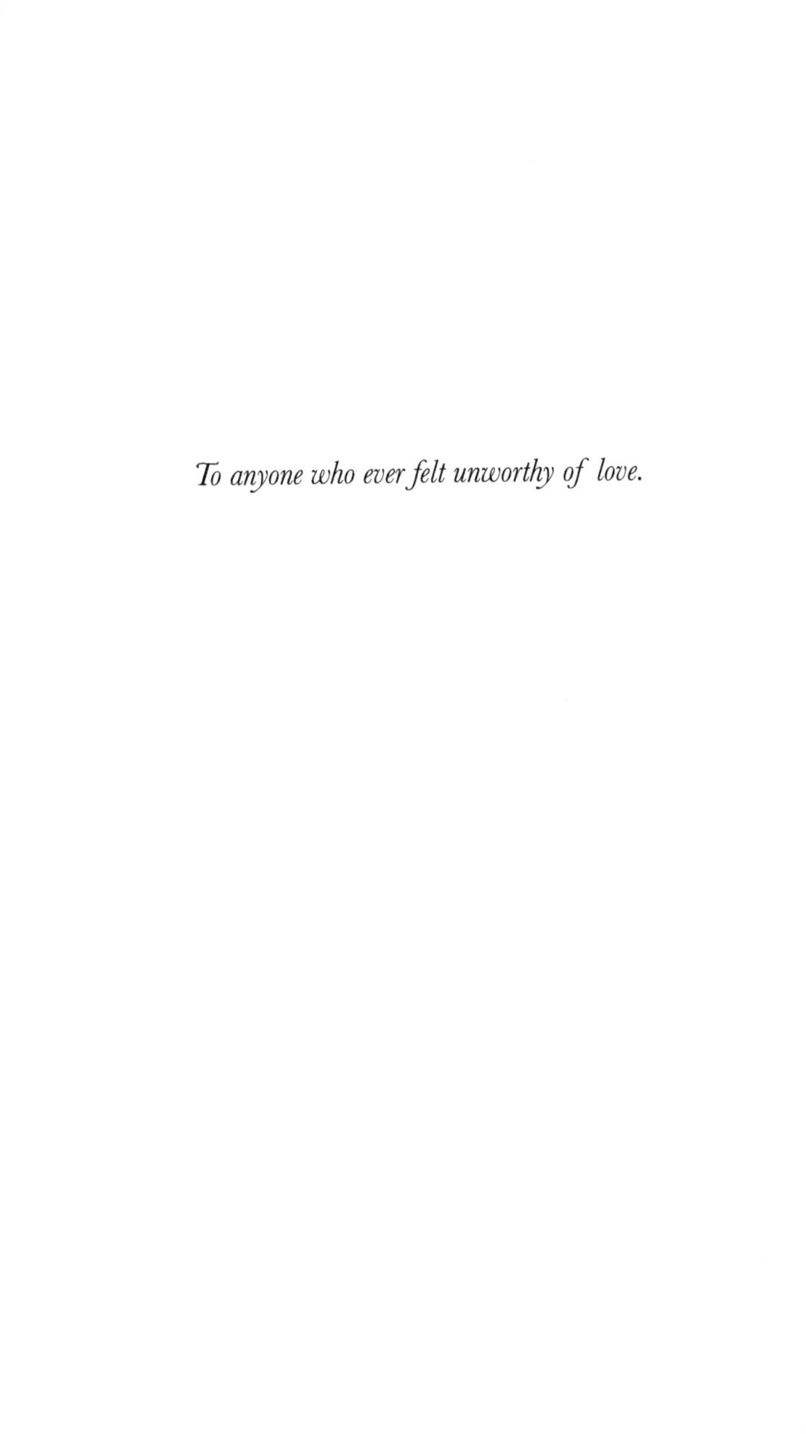

To anyone who ever felt unworthy of love.

CHAPTER I

The droning, inane gossip flitting around the room had Kevah suppressing a groan of boredom.

Ms. Morgan, dripping in glittering fabrics, whispered not-so-quietly from behind her umpteenth drink. "He hasn't shown his face since the girl was born."

Mr. Gugpont shook his head, scanning the crowd while looking down his long nose at all who weren't part of their conversation. "Of course not. I heard from the latest employer of the midwife who attended the birth that she told his maid the child had *gray eyes*. You know what that means."

Ms. Morgan tutted. "Kinetic," she sneered. "You know, I have nothing against Kinetics, of course not, but the chances of one being born to two Fire Wielders? Well… we all know the odds of that." She held up her hand, warding off nonexistent judgment. "I know, I know, it's possible. But what are the odds?"

Kevah downed his drink, not caring what it contained. The contents burned his throat, warming him from the inside. He only half listened to the rumors constantly circulating at such tedious parties.

All those wealthy nobles with businesses to run, and they had nothing better to do than stand around gossiping. All while wearing the finest clothing the City of Shifters offered and drinking the most expensive magic-infused liquor they could import from the City of Witches.

Another woman in their group leaned in, lowering her voice as though she were revealing something heinous. "*I* heard from the neighbor's gardener that she glimpsed the child through the window playing with something dark and transparent."

Ms. Morgan and Mr. Gugpont gasped in unison at the new information, hands flying to their chests to protect the jewels hanging there. Kevah, usually incapable of caring about the latest gossip, found his ears perking up, eager to hear any news about the rumored child. Lady Aladonna had been working to shut down that particular branch of the rumor mill, but the attempts were obviously unsuccessful.

"Not a Kinetic then."

"*Shadow Spinner.*"

In unison, they all turned to Kevah as if suddenly remembering his presence on the fringe of their group. They all shifted, discretely widening the distance between themselves and him. None of them met his eye, but they all waited patiently for his input.

If anyone would know, it would be him.

Kevah clenched his jaw, biting back irritation at their discomfort, and sifted through everything he'd heard regarding the rumors of the Dark Magic child instead. As heir to the lordship of the Elementals, Kevah attended every meeting and event hosted by Lady Aladonna. He knew the inner workings of the city as well as anyone. If the next Shadow Spinner had been born in the City of Elementals, especially to an influential Elemental family, he should know about it.

Except he didn't.

Like everyone else, he'd heard the rumors; they all had, but there was no proof yet. The parents hadn't brought the baby forward for execution, and short of taking the child into custody for observation, there was nothing the city could do.

The family had abandoned all social obligations since the child's birth. They claimed the mother, a kind-hearted woman with gorgeous red hair, had experienced a difficult birth and was still recovering—a plausible enough excuse.

Kevah plastered on his most neutral and practiced smile, hoping it met his eyes. "As of right now, we cannot confirm or deny rumors of the Dark Magic child; however, should we learn of anything concrete, rest assured the child will be… dealt with."

That pleased the three gossips, and they quickly changed subjects.

"Anyway." Ms. Morgan leaned in close, placing a hesitant hand on Kevah's arm, peering up at him with what he assumed she intended to be sultry eyes. Instead, they only read as uncertain. "People have been wondering if you'll take a lady when you claim the lordship?" Batting her makeup-coated eyelashes at him, she trailed a trembling finger up his arm.

Kevah got the sense she was trying not to yank her hand away in fear despite her attempts at winning his favor.

Kevah suppressed a disgusted grimace. That complicated dynamic wasn't uncommon at such events. Women made advances toward him, hoping to win his favor, but few were sure they wanted it. Winning his heart would mean becoming the next Lady of Elementals, which came with untold riches and a seat among the most influential in Thaumoria. Inciting his contempt, however… well, he wasn't sure what they thought would happen, but it wasn't good.

Kevah had never fed into those fears, but dispelling them, he learned, was impossible. A reputation that wasn't his preceded him, and he could do nothing about it. Typically, he tried to play along with their wavering flirtations, placating them while gently letting them down, but it wasn't easy when those women in question were three times his age.

Patting the woman's hand, he stepped away from her wrinkled touch. "Unfortunately, I have not found the right person. But I assure you, when I do, you'll be the first to know."

He lifted her hand to his lips and kissed her knuckles. She breathed a sigh of relief at his rejection, but her cheeks blushed all the same. Turning away, she fanned herself with her free hand to hide her reaction.

Kevah excused himself, hiding how he wiped away the lingering feel of her hand in his way.

Smoothly, he finished another drink and exchanged his empty glass with a full one as a server passed. He weaved between party guests, putting on his most charming smile and nodding at those who greeted him, which seemed to be everyone.

No one wanted to risk offending the lord-to-be by ignoring him.

An arm hooked around his neck, barreling into his side and knocking him off balance.

"Oh, you and Ms. Morgan sure make a cute couple. I'm glad you finally found yourself a nice girl." Malak slurred into his ear.

Kevah reached up and pushed Malak's face away from his, dislodging himself from the embrace. Scowling, Kevah downed another drink in a single gulp. The room around him fuzzed at the edges, but it wouldn't be until it was spinning like a cyclone that he would even begin to enjoy himself.

"Yeah, thanks a lot, jackass. You were supposed to save me if I got caught up in one of the gossip bubbles with the old biddies."

Malak barked a laugh that was too loud to be polite and downed his drink. Before Kevah could protest, Malak confiscated his empty glass and exchanged them for full ones as a server passed, nearly knocking over the tray's entire array of sparkling wines.

"You two looked so good together I couldn't bring myself to step in. Truly, I think you've found the one. And when she dies in fifteen years, you can find the next one."

Kevah rolled his eyes, turned away from Malak, and scanned the crowd, looking for someone closer to his age to entertain him for the evening. His gaze jumped around the room, skimming from one familiar girl to another.

Rolling his neck, he tried to crack away the tedium building between his shoulder blades.

It is always the same people at these incestuous parties.

Malak gestured with his drink at a familiar Anima with her hair twisted up into a puff of curls upon her head, talking with Kevah's mother. "I say you go for Hazel."

Kevah shook his head. "No way. That's already happened, what? Five times? Any more, and she'll get the wrong idea."

He opted not to mention how, after the

last banal party, where he snuck off with the estate's newest Witch, Lady Aladonna insisted there would be no more one-night stands. Such behavior was unbecoming of an up-and-coming leader, she'd told him—or so he assumed. He hadn't been listening.

The monotonous music swelled to a crescendo, couples swirling to the beat. Kevah hummed along with the orchestra, tapping his fingers against his glass in time with the drums.

Through the moving bodies, a glimpse of a golden woman caught his attention.

She was someone unique.

Someone *different.*

CHAPTER 2

Every nerve in Kevah's body came alive.

The monster that he fought so hard not to be reared its head, eager for the next hunt. For the freshest challenge.

Kevah took another swig of his drink and pushed the half-empty glass into Malak's hand. "Don't wait up."

Malak downed Kevah's drink without a second thought. "Go get her, man."

Kevah pulled himself up to his full height, adjusted his embroidered jacket, and ran a dark hand through his long red hair. He stalked the dance floor, avoiding fluttering hems and leering eyes.

He never took his gaze off the rare beauty clad in shimmering fabric, a carnal need building within him. She casually hung off the arm of a prominent businessman Kevah couldn't remember the name of, her hand resting in the crease of his elbow.

People moved out of Kevah's way as he wove between them, giving him quick, polite nods. Soon, he found himself by her side, pulling the focus of the conversation away from whatever subject they had been discussing.

The small group hushed at his presence, but their awed expressions turned eager with a hint of unease. They were pleased to be graced with his attention but wary of saying the wrong thing.

"Kevah, how wonderful of you to join us," cooed a Witch wrapped in deep indigo, only a slight waver to their words.

He graced them with a polite smile, ignoring how uncomfortable they had become, before turning his attention to the target of his desire.

Her golden-flecked gaze swept over him, assessing him from top to bottom, taking in every detail but never revealing her thoughts.

The urge to lean in and brush his fingers along her bare arm was almost overwhelming. The air around her drew Kevah in, daring him to whisk her away and sweep her off her feet like he had with dozens of other women.

And then her features flattened, unimpressed by what she saw. "May I help you?"

The cold words froze Kevah where he stood. They were as disinterested as her flat glare, almost… irritated by his presence.

The man she hung on blanched, aware of the inappropriate (and potentially dangerous) encounter he was witnessing. As if Kevah might smite him just for being associated with the woman.

The group's paling faces around him either blatantly stared at the woman or tried to look at anything but her. With a single question, every one of them became embarrassed by the company they held, but they weren't willing to leave for fear of being rude.

Kevah disregarded them all, completely entranced. He had somehow waded into unfamiliar waters, and his heart raced at the prospect of it, eager for the challenge.

The woman didn't fear him in the least.

Kevah abhorred that so many were afraid of him based on a history that wasn't his, walking on eggshells the moment they noticed him nearby, but he'd grown used to it over the years. He had even used it to his advantage when it pleased him, such as persuading any woman he wished to join him in bed. The woman's distaste excited him, however. The boldness of it. She was someone he wanted to know.

The music dipped, leading into an upbeat melody he knew well.

"Dance with me," he requested.

Her hard, glittering eyes prickled, flashing an emotion he couldn't quite decipher—something akin to disgust at the suggestion.

Looking away, returning to her group, she

threw a rejection over her shoulder. "I don't think so."

The man at her side visibly flinched. Sweat beaded his forehead, and he dabbed it with a handkerchief. The others made nervous gestures—fixing hair, shifting, smoothing a non-existent wrinkle on their attire. But Kevah's breath caught, delighted by her refusal.

The only person who'd ever denied him anything was Lady Aladonna. Her rejection threw him off kilter in the best way.

He captured her fingers in his, boldly pulling them to his chest.

Leaning close, he pled low and husky, "Please. Just one dance."

Her eyes bounced from him to his fingers and back. Her cold expression didn't change, but the loathing in her eyes became more akin to trepidation.

She swallowed hard, glancing around at how many watched.

"I'm sure there is another—" she started, but the man beside her cut in.

"She'd love to!"

She whipped around to give the sweaty Witch a withering stare, but he implored her with his eyes, silently begging her to agree.

"Fine," she sighed, giving a slight nod.

That nod was all Kevah needed. All he wanted. His smile widened until it split his face, triumph swelling in his chest as he pulled her away and onto the dance floor.

Lifting her hand, he spun her beneath his arm so they could seamlessly flow into the couples already on the floor. Her full skirt lifted, wrapping around their legs, engulfing them in a cloud of gold that matched her blonde hair falling over a bare shoulder.

Kevah pulled her close, and she placed a delicate hand in his, the other picking up the glittering hem of her dress. Hesitantly, he placed a gentle hand on her waist.

He simultaneously didn't want to scare her off and wanted to test the boundaries of her irritation. Her lack of unease was both refreshing and enthralling. When she didn't flee at his touch, he stepped to the beat thumping around them.

Stiff in his arms, she danced as gracefully

as a wooden board, glancing at her feet as he led her around the floor. The corner of his mouth lifted, amused.

"You don't know this dance, do you?"

Her head snapped up, cold eyes narrowing as they challenged him. "Of course I do."

Kevah couldn't control the amusement growing inside him. He was a child testing the limits of a parent's patience, wanting to see how far he could push his luck.

But then the toe of her shoe caught on the floor, sending her tripping into his arms. Years of training honed his reflexes, and he caught her before she fell, turning the stumbling into a quick spin.

"I thought all nobles learned this dance by the time they could walk," he teased.

She glared at him, holding her chin high. "Not all of us grew up in a wealthy home with nothing to do but learn to dance."

The words slapped him across the face, making him pull back to distance himself from her venomous mouth. Kevah's desire to push her annoyance died with his realization. Of all people, he understood what it was like to catch up to noble standards. When Malak was learning to waltz from his tycoon parents, Kevah still lived in the city's center, kicking rocks at makeshift targets in a nearby alley.

But that was before his life at the estate. Before his parents handed him over to Lady Aladonna to be raised as the next lord. Practically another life altogether.

Her words exposed what her cold, golden-flecked eyes shielded. They bounced around the room, not necessarily out of distaste for him, but to ensure no one saw her trip. She was trying to blend in, and his invitation to dance drew attention to a shortcoming she didn't want revealed.

"You're right. I'm sorry," he whispered, low enough only she would hear.

Studying his face, scrutinizing his sincerity, she squared her shoulders, regaining her pride.

Adjusting his grip, he guided her with his hands and tried his best to lead her unyielding body to the beat. "Relax a little, and let me lead you. The song is almost over. I promise I won't let you fall."

After a brief contemplation, she took a deep breath and nodded. Brows furrowing, she set her jaw and stared at his chest as though trying to look through him. But, muscle by muscle, she relaxed into his touch. It seemed almost painful for her to relinquish the slightest control. Within moments, though, he had them swaying to a less complicated step. With each strike of the drums, she grew more confident he wouldn't embarrass her.

The song hit its crescendo, each note amplified by the Kinetics around the room, using their magic to manipulate the vibrations forming the melody. The woman's eyes met his again, but some of the iciness had melted, and he fell deep into their frigid embrace. He lost himself, the rest of the party fading away until only the two of them were spinning around the dance floor.

Nothing mattered but the beauty in his arms. The feel of her in his arms was intoxicating. Like she was an Air Wielder stealing his breath, creating a whirlwind just for them.

He tipped his head closer, wanting to bridge the gap between them and press his full lips to hers, wondering if they were softer than her eyes.

And for a moment, he thought she'd meet him halfway. Not because she feared the repercussions if she didn't, the way every other woman he'd taken to bed had, but because he intrigued her too.

When the last note hit and the song ended, she pulled out of his arms and beelined for the exit.

CHAPTER 3

Desperate for her to stay, Kevah followed his reluctant dance partner. If nothing else, he wanted to get her name.

Pushing between partygoers, half-heartedly apologizing as he went, he glimpsed her through the crowd. People flowed around her like water around a fish without noticing they were doing it at all. They all seemed to move on instinct. A step to the left so she could pass, then a step back, as if nothing had happened.

Kevah caught up to her as she broke the edge of the partygoers, catching her wrist.

"Please, don't go," he pled quietly, trying not to draw attention.

"I did not come here to be bedded a lord-to-be," she snarled.

On instinct, he opened his mouth to lie, to tell her he intended no such thing. All he wanted was to get to know her. All his usual lines flew to the tip of his tongue, but she cut him off with a sharp look.

"Don't you dare lie to me," she bit.

Kevah snapped his mouth shut, taken aback. Once again, he was unsure how to react and intrigued by her indifference to who he was.

They stared at each other for a drawn-out moment, a battle of silent wills, until a regal voice cut through the thickening air around them. "Kevah, dear, leaving so soon?"

Those metallic-flecked eyes before him widened a hair, panic flickering across them.

Kevah took only a heartbeat to regain his composure before turning to find Lady Aladonna approaching them.

If Thaumoria had queens, they'd aspire to be such a magnificent and imposing sight.

Head held high, shoulders pulled back, utterly sure of who she was and the power she wielded, Lady Aladonna glided across the ballroom, a river moving with ease around the comparatively graceless boulders that were her guests.

Lady Aladonna was the only person in Thaumoria who had ever put Kevah in his place growing up. Although he'd won private training duels for years, he still couldn't imagine himself filling her shoes as the head of the Elemental City. She was too resplendent. Too wicked smart for her own good. And soon enough, Kevah would take her place.

"No, of course not." He tipped his head in a polite bow. "I was simply showing a friend out."

Lady Aladonna's ocean-blue eyes grazed over the golden woman hiding behind his shoulder. Her lips tilted into a satisfied smile. "I see. And who might this be?"

A name found itself on the forefront of Kevah's tongue, leaving his lips before he could second guess it. "Atana, my lady."

Kevah's brows twitched into something like confusion before he forced them smooth again.

Where in the world had *that* come from? By the Gods and Goddesses, he hoped that was her real name.

Atana gave a slight curtsey at the sound of her supposed name, bowing her head so as not to draw attention.

Lady Aladonna thoughtfully hummed, appraising the two standing so close. "Hmm. I'd hate to see you leaving so soon, my dear. Assure me Kevah has not scared you off with his atrocious dancing."

Atana's lips twitched at the corners, though she continued to stare at the hem of Aladonna's skirt. "No, not all, my Lady."

There was a suggestive but warning gleam in Aladonna's eyes as they flitted back and forth between them. *Court, do not seduce,* they seemed to say to him.

It wasn't required for the lord or lady of Elementals to take a partner; Lady Aladonna certainly hadn't. Kevah always theorized she couldn't stand to share her metaphorical throne. But she believed Kevah was too wild, and the right woman would ground him before he came to power. Clearly, she was picturing Atana as that person—the person Atana clearly didn't want to be.

"I apologize, my lady; I think you misunderstood. I was going to show Atana the gardens."

Atana shot him a look, boring into the side of his head, but he hoped she saw how he was trying to save her. The gardens housed a handful of discreet escapes from the estate. If he could get her out there, he could help her escape into the night without causing a scene.

Lady Aladonna smiled gently. "Ah," she sighed, "the gardens. They are the most beautiful part of the estate, maintained by the best Earth Wielders and Witches the city has to offer. Please do enjoy yourself."

With one last scrutinizing glance at Kevah, Aladonna melted back into the crowd.

Kevah turned away, leading Atana with a hand on her elbow. She followed reluctantly, glancing around to see how many people were watching them slip away to be alone.

"What was that? I have no interest in *seeing the gardens* with you." Her blazing, brilliant eyes bore into him, staring him down without hesitation.

It captivated him, pulling his practiced, placating smile into an ear-to-ear grin.

Something about her reminded him of a storm at sea—fierce, unrelenting, and yet simultaneously breathtaking. She was a force to be reckoned with, and he was eager to meet it head-on.

"I know, but if you left this early, she'd take it as an insult. This way, I can show you a way out, and she'll be none the wiser." Taking her hand in his, he hooked it through his arm to appear more intimate.

Atana huffed but didn't argue or pull away.

Kevah glimpsed Malak drunkenly flirting with a beautiful Water Wielder woman with abyss-black hair and brilliant blue eyes who seemed utterly unimpressed by his incoherently slurred flattery. Inwardly, he wished his only friend the best of luck.

Kevah and Atana walked silently until

they reached the glass double doors, cloaked in lustrous fabrics, that led to the gardens.

Two guards stood on either side, opening the doors for them in a grand exit. Kevah always found guards on the estate grounds humorous, given that two of the most powerful people in Thaumoria lived within those walls, but that wasn't his call to make.

Arm in arm, he and Atana strode into the cool night air. Kevah took his first easy breath of the night, drinking in the brackish breeze blowing off the city's seaports in the distance.

"What's your actual name?" he asked once they'd created a suitable distance between themselves and the guards to avoid being overheard.

Atana glanced at him from the corner of her eye before turning her attention back to the passing bushes, as if trying to decide whether to tell him the truth. "It is Atana. You guessed correctly."

Guessed didn't seem like an accurate description of what had happened. "How is that possible?"

She shrugged so casually he almost

believed it was that simple. "I guess I'm just one of those whose face fits their name."

Kevah snorted a laugh. "Yes, that must be it."

Pulling them to a stop beneath an ivy-covered arch, he stepped away, presenting himself for inspection with arms open wide and a playful grin. "Tell me, does my name fit my face?"

The corner of her lips twitched, almost amused, but not quite. Crossing her arms, she tilted her head to the side and studied him from head to toe, really looking at him for the first time that night.

From his long, bright red hair, sea-blue eyes, soil-brown skin, and lanky limbs, he was an odd combination of features she took her time analyzing. Her scrutiny was palpable, like fingers grazing his bare skin. He was grateful for his jacket, hiding the goosebumps that appeared wherever her gaze touched.

"Kevah," she breathed as though trying it out for the first time. She drew out each letter, tasting how they moved from the back of the throat to the front of the lips.

Watching her thin lips move, he wondered what his name would taste like as it slid along her tongue. Wondered what she'd look like when she let down those cold, icy walls. To see just a flicker of warmth behind those golden eyes. To see her lounged in his bed, lips parted in a moan, features relaxed with ecstasy…

"No," she pronounced, breaking him out of his fantasy. "I don't think it suits you."

Blinking, he tried to remember what they were talking about. His name. Right.

Feigning disappointment, he let his hands fall to his side. "Well… perhaps you could suggest an alternative."

She looked him over again, toying with him, then shrugged. "I think 'lordling' will do for now."

Pressing his lips together, he suppressed the urge to contest that title. Lordling somehow felt even worse than "heir" or the foreboding "lord." But he could tell she was trying to get a rise out of him, poking fun at his reluctance to embrace his position, so instead he offered his arm to her again. "Of course. Shall we continue?"

She smirked but retook his arm without hesitation, and his chest swelled with just a hint of pride, instantly forgiving the new nickname. He tried to hide his triumphant smile, but it was a wasted effort.

They continued beneath a series of latticed arches covered in emerald leaves laced with small white flowers that glowed in the moonlight.

On the other side of the latticed tunnel, colorful bushes full of flowers greeted them. Each one had been specifically selected, whether for its aesthetics, its medicinal properties, or both. There wasn't a plant in the estate that didn't have a purpose. Atana ran a finger along the petals as they passed. Silky petals of purples, blues, pinks, and yellows slid beneath her fingertips.

"Are you from here? The City of Elementals?" he asked.

She considered the question for a long time. Long enough for the flowers to end, turning to hedges around them as they entered a small, simple maze. "No. No, I'm not."

He watched her from the corner of his eye, but she only watched the bushes as they passed. They'd soon envelop them, tall, green, and pruned to perfection.

"Where did you grow up?" It seemed like a safe question—casual and easy—but she hesitated.

Her expression was far too composed and controlled to show her reluctance, but it hung around them like the perfume of flowers, thick in the night air.

Patiently, he waited.

Finally, she answered, "The City of Shifters."

Of the four cities she could've said, that was the last one he expected. Her stoicism was far more characteristic of Witches or Kinetics. Shifters were passionate people who lived for their art. They believed in self-expression and embracing their differences—nothing like the ethereal creature on his arm.

"That's… interesting."

He hoped she'd continue talking and elaborate on her past and childhood, but she didn't. They progressed through the gardens, listening to the symphony of insects singing around them.

When they reached the back of the garden, Kevah led them to a spot in the wall he knew well. There the foliage was less cared for, wilder, like Kevah himself. Far from the curious eyes of any guests who might wander into the gardens during a party, no one bothered to keep the area perfect. Large trees lined the wall, their trunks slightly warped and knotted, perfect for a curious child to climb in search of bird nests.

He called upon his Earth Wielding, using both hands to push against a section of the stone wall. With little effort on his part, the seamless door slid open as if on hinges. While the wall was massive, at least four times as tall as he was, and impossible to climb, a handful of loose sections would open at an Earth Wielder's command. A little-known piece of knowledge he kept close to his heart.

Kevah gestured at the narrow opening. "As promised. Few guard this section since it is far from known entrances. It will be easy for you to slip away unnoticed."

Atana eyed the opening before looking up at him, round eyes almost approving. He thought she might say something verging on appreciative or even offer to stay, but instead, she started toward the opening.

Kevah felt her slipping through his fingers, away into the night, never to be seen again, and he couldn't let her go. He reached out, taking her hand loosely so she could pull out of his grip if she wished.

But she paused, letting him keep her just a moment longer.

"Please, stay."

Holding his gaze, her breath quickened as she contemplated his request. "Why?"

That was an excellent question.

Kevah had his pick of women throughout the city. None were brave enough to reject him, and most fought to win his heart despite the danger he posed. He could walk away and find a new flirtation within the hour. But none would intrigue him the way she did. None of them would stare unflinchingly into the depths of his soul and challenge him with such cold grace. She didn't care that he was the heir to the lordship, nor was she intimidated by his power. Even his parents hesitated to challenge his wishes, fearing what he might be capable of.

And yet, there she was. Unaffected. Unimpressed. Unflinching.

It thrilled him.

"Because I get the sense that you are unlike anyone else in Thaumoria, and it is intoxicating."

A blush crept over the tips of her ears, but there was something almost sad about how her shoulders fell.

"Never have truer words been spoken," she whispered, as if she didn't mean for him to hear them.

"Then you'll stay? I want to learn everything you're willing to share."

She scoffed and looked at the green grass between their feet. "If you learned everything there was about me, you'd have me thrown out by dawn."

The words seemed to come from a wound so deep within her it never saw the light of day. Kevah wanted to wipe away that insecurity. He wanted the fierceness—the woman who had, until that point, shown nothing but borderline disdain for him.

So he put on his most obnoxious, arrogant smirk. "Is that a challenge? Because, as an heir, I've been training for challenges my whole life."

Atana rolled her golden eyes, but the faintest smile graced her lips, amused at his pompous declaration.

"No, lordling. It was not a challenge, but a promise." The words were sarcastic, as though meant to wound him, but she didn't hurl them with near the venom as before.

"Then you'll stay?" He tugged her back into the garden, away from the outside world.

Her chin lifted, a coy look filling her eyes, but she stepped back into the garden, letting him guide her away from the wall. "We'll see."

CHAPTER 4

Reaching out with his Earth Wielding, Kevah shut the stone door, sealing off the outside world. Atana retook his arm without prompting, and Kevah's heart lifted.

They stepped back into the maze of bushes, striding between pruned foliage.

"Until dawn to learn everything about you," Kevah mused, wondering where to begin.

"Until dawn to learn how mistaken you are to pursue me," she corrected.

"Until dawn to win your favor."

Atana shook her head, rolling her eyes again. "If you'd like to look at it that way."

Until dawn… that only gave Kevah about six hours. Any other time, six hours in the company of the Elemental City's elite would have seemed like a lifelong prison sentence. Instead, it felt like an executioner's sentence. As they wordlessly wound down the path, the minutes dwindled before his eyes, sand slipping through an hourglass.

Before, he couldn't wait for the ball to end, and the minutes seemed to drag on. Time sped up, and he didn't want the night to end. For the first time in his life, he questioned just how powerful he truly was if even he couldn't stop the sun from rising.

"So… tell me about the gentleman you came with." Kevah started, eager to dive headfirst into the mystery that was Atana.

She smirked. "Lee Maccob. Not much to tell."

Maccob… Kevah thought he recognized the man. He was a Witch who made a small fortune by selling overpriced cosmetics to the wealthiest Elemental nobles, guaranteeing specialized anti-aging magic. Based on what Kevah saw of those who swore by the products, they were rather ineffective.

"I see, and you two are involved?" The feral monster within him, the one he fought so hard to starve, salivated at the thought. It enjoyed the idea of stealing the beauty beside him away from another, like a pirate pilfering a precious gold coin.

Kevah led them through the maze, moving on instinct. He had memorized every route through the garden long ago, when he was a child running a wreck through the grounds, pushing the ever-growing limits of his magic. He'd leave boulder-sized craters beneath his feet, pull water drops from flower petals to spray at the gardeners, and set fire to the bushes when he laughed. Kevah had been out of control, free, and learned every inch of the grounds.

Atana shrugged. "We have... an understanding."

Kevah raised a curious eyebrow. "What exactly does that mean?"

She didn't answer right away, chewing on her lip in thought.

A grand four-tier fountain appeared, the ever-flowing water sparkling in the full moon's light. The base was round, nearly twice as wide as Kevah was tall. Each tier represented an element, with stone columns on the bottom, followed by a tier of carved flames. The next were delicate swirls that looked like they should've crumpled under the weight of the sculpted waves forming the final tier.

Atana pulled away from Kevah's arm, sat on the fountain's edge, and dragged her fingers through the clear water.

"After his wife passed away a year ago, Lee found his sales dwindling. He felt that a beautiful woman on his arm would be the publicity he needed. I attend functions at his side, and he provides me with a comfortable life."

Kevah would've felt bad for her, reduced to nothing but a walking advertisement, if not for the conspiratorial curl of her lips and the coy glint in her eye.

He stepped closer. "But you two are not a couple?"

She snorted, watching water drip from her fingertips. "Of course not. He is far too… insubstantial. However, he is suitable for now."

For now…

Drawn by the ambition beneath her words, he moved closer. There was something almost… savage about how she spoke of her situation with Maccob. As if, while he thought he was using her, in reality, she was using him. The subtlety of it was captivating.

As if realizing she'd shared too much, she pressed her lips together, turning her gold-flecked gaze on him. "Anyway, fair is fair, lordling. I can't do all the talking tonight. Tell me about life among the elite."

She was deflecting; that much was clear, but Kevah was eager to please. He sat beside her on the fountain's base, leaving mere inches between them.

"My life is wholly uninteresting, I assure you." Atana cocked her head, and Kevah chuckled. "Ok, it's not too bad. The travel is quite interesting, visiting cities around Thaumoria and meeting with the other leaders. The meetings themselves are rather dull, but the cities are fascinating."

A wistful sigh escaped her as she watched the water fall. "The snow-capped mountains surrounding the Kinetic City are supposed to be…"

"Enchanting," Kevah finished for her, leaning ever closer, drawn in by each new detail he learned.

She met his gaze for a heartbeat before pulling away and smoothing her skirts. "Yes, something like that." She cleared her throat, the icy mask falling back into place.

But she'd let it slip for a moment. Kevah saw something beneath that cold exterior: a desire, a dream. Something more than disdain for him and his existence beside her. He wanted more.

Rubbing his palms together, he tried to find a question that would reveal a little more. "So, what does a comfortable life beside Maccob entail? Are your days filled with never-ending parties and events?"

Rolling her head to the side, she sighed. It

was frustrated rather than wistful, though. "That *is* wholly uninteresting."

"You must fill your days with something."

"I enjoy… studying." She said the word like a secret. Something that hid a wealth of information.

"Studying cosmetics?" he teased.

A corner of her mouth lifted. "People."

Stunned, he opened and closed his mouth, unsure of what to say next. "Excuse me?"

She laughed, an electric sound he felt in his core. "People. They are fascinating. I find myself intrigued by why people do the things they do. How they navigate social situations, why they choose political affiliations, etc. Psychology and whatnot."

"And how does one *study* people?"

That coy gleam surfaced again as she watched him from the corner of her eye. "Oh, trust me. I have my ways."

They fell into a comfortable silence as he watched her, and she watched the falling water. He couldn't pull his eyes away. There was nothing more captivating, nothing more alluring. If only he could touch her, run his fingers along her jaw and down her neck. He wanted to hear her gasp as he pressed a kiss to the sensitive spots there——

Water droplets hit his face. He jumped, wiping his eyes clear.

"Watch those thoughts, lordling." Despite the way she scolded him, he could hear the smile in her words.

"You don't know what I was thinking."

She lifted a single eyebrow. "It was written across your face."

He scoffed. "I don't know what you're talking about."

Her fingers dipped into the water again, threatening to spray him like a cat in heat. "What did I tell you about lying to me?"

He laughed, using his magic to shake away the remaining water dripping from his nose.

"I was just thinking that… it would be my pleasure to show you the library," he lied. "The estate has an expansive section on psychology."

"You spin stories like yarn." Fingers flicking, she sent water droplets flying at him again.

However, he was prepared. Without looking away, Kevah hardly dipped into his vast stores of magic to stop each droplet in midair, crystalizing them as they froze. With a wave of his hand, the crystals spread around them, creating dancing diamonds and catching the moonlight.

Most Water Wielders would've needed a lot of concentration to perform such an action. But for Kevah, it was as easy as breathing. His elements were an extension of him, bowing to his every desire.

Atana's breath caught in her throat, eyes widening just a hair at his rare show of power. Everyone knew how he easily commanded his elements; few had ever witnessed it.

Caught in a moment, the world slowed around them just so they could have a second together, surrounded by the night.

"Storytelling is only one of my many talents, my lady." The words came out low, from somewhere deep in his chest—a place he rarely found outside the bedroom.

Her lips parted, her words breathy even as she tried to sound cold. "Is that so?"

Kevah leaned in closer, the tips of their noses brushing. "Would you like to see?"

Biting her lip, he thought she might lean in. Give in to him the way so many did.

"Yes," she breathed, "I'd enjoy seeing the library immensely."

Pulling back, she jumped to her feet, her full skirts fanning around her as she walked away.

Pressing his lips together hard, he let out a long, frustrated breath that rumbled in his chest like a growl. The surrounding crystals thawed in response, falling to the ground like rain.

When his eyes found her again, a cruel smirk greeted him. She knew exactly what she was doing, drawing him in and pushing him away like the rising tide of the seaports.

Kevah gave himself a single breath to compose himself before finding his way to her side once again.

"Shall we then?" He offered her his arm.

She took it, lifting her chin triumphantly. "Lead the way."

CHAPTER 5

Kevah led them down hallway after hallway, taking the longest route he could think of to avoid any straying guests. He wanted to keep Atana to himself.

"Why are there so many… rocks?" she asked, hinting at a chuckle beneath her words.

They passed another alcove graced with a display of precious gems and stones that Kevah had brought back from his travels.

"They're mine. I collect them."

She raised an eyebrow at him.

He sighed. "When I was younger, Lady Aladonna dragged me around Thaumoria to attend my first conferences with other leaders. I was bored out of my mind. When it became clear that my boredom often manifested as playing with fire, Lady Aladonna tried redirecting my focus. So, she'd tell me to find rocks. Apparently, she assumed a feral Earth Wielding child was safer than a bored Fire Wielding child.

"Only, it became a genuine hobby. Walking barefoot around the outskirts of the cities, I sensed the different materials beneath my feet, buried deep within the earth. So I'd dig them up and bring them home. Now…" He shrugged.

Atana took a while to respond. "Playing… with *fire*?"

Kevah bit his lip, heat creeping up his neck. "Flames are quite beautiful and fascinating, especially to a child. However, others tend not to agree when you scorch tapestries because you were setting off sparks during a trade agreement. The Anima Mother did *not* find that so cute."

Atana pressed her lips into a thin line, shoulders shaking with a suppressed laugh.

Kevah's embarrassment faded away with the pride of glimpsing what could be when she let him in. He wanted more. More laughs, more smiles, more warmth from her.

Seeing the library doors gave him hope he would see just that.

The metal handles were cool and well-worn in Kevah's hands. Dulled by the hands of generations of lords and ladies before him.

He ushered Atana inside, closing the door behind him with a soft thud and cutting them off from the rest of the estate.

Atana sucked in a small gasp, her only visible reaction to the private library within.

Although it wasn't the largest of the two libraries on the estate, it was by far Kevah's favorite.

The entire two-story room was a labor of love, made of painstakingly carved stone. So much of the estate's beautiful architecture resulted from Shifters using their magic to craft unforgettable art into the building itself. But this library? There was no doubt in his mind that Elementals had crafted it.

Sometimes, he'd close his eyes and place

his hands on one of the stone railings. He swore he could feel the Elemental magic layered upon it. Woven into the very being of the rock, touched by only the most powerful. The magic in the air lingered on his tongue, hanging alongside the scent of old books and dust. There was no water in the room, but how the stone curved reminded him of the ripples in a wave and rivers cutting canyons. Moving with the grace of streams, the way so many Water Wielders did.

And then the fire… all around the library were sconces, also carved from stone. The entire estate had electricity, as did most of the wealthiest residents of Thaumoria, but they never used it in that library.

The private library of the Elemental Lords and Ladies was a place for the purest elements.

Kevah waved a hand through the air, calling upon the fire living in his veins. As his hand swept through the air in an arc, flame followed, alighting every corner of the library, filling every sconce and roaring to life in the fireplace on the far side of the room.

Beside him, Atana's lips parted, her fingers brushing against them in awe as she drifted to the center of the room. Firelight caught the glittering strands of her gown flickering as she spun, taking in the room.

"It's… amazing. You can *feel* the magic in here."

" 'Like the salt in the air,' " Kevah answered, quoting a passage from one of his favorite childhood books. " 'Like the salt in the air, magic lingered across the land.' "

" 'It lifted her spirits as they soared higher, breaking through the clouds until it was only the two of them together against the world,' " Atana continued, finishing the passage.

Kevah grinned, finding his way to her side. "You've read it."

It wasn't a question, but Atana nodded. "Who hasn't? *The Tale of a Girl Who Rode a Dragon*. That's hard for a child to pass up."

Watching her take in the library entranced Kevah. He leaned in, drinking in the air around her. His heart leaped when her gaze met his, an unhindered smile on her lips, the first genuine smile he'd seen.

"Growing up in the City of Shifters, I would have thought you'd be used to beautiful spaces." Kevah remembered his first trip to the City of Shifters. He'd been in awe the entire time. Their city reflected their main export perfectly: art. Each building was unique, with bright colors and one-of-a-kind architecture around every corner. As beautiful as this library was, he had to admit that it couldn't compare to where she grew up.

Her lips thinned, gaze going distant as if visiting that far-off city.

"It's not the same. The art there is commonplace, almost essential. It feels less… inspired. People are always looking to make the next best thing. But this…" Her hands lifted and fell as if gesturing to the entire library. "This was an act of love and desire— something just for those who made it. You can feel that in the rock. In the air."

Looking around, Kevah saw the library in a different light. He always assumed it was just a little slice of her world. But he saw it as its own thing for the first time. Something extraordinary that only existed for the lords, ladies, and now, her. It made him stand a little taller, his grin widening, proud that he had thought to bring her there. Until he looked back down and her eyes were still hazy, glimpsing something far away in the south.

He wanted the smile back—the wit and the life that seemed to emanate from her.

"Come. I think you'll like this." He took her fingers in his and led her to an alcove shadowed by an overhanging balcony.

Two flaming sconces on either side of the nook created dancing shadows, just enough light to read by. A round table, piled high with his most recent reads, stood there. A podium kept precariously at the table's edge held an open tome. Splayed across the pages was a detailed illustrated map of Thaumoria.

Atana tentatively stepped up to it, skimming her fingers along the edge of the pages, barely brushing the delicate paper as if it would crumble at her touch. She stared longingly at the shaded hills and valleys surrounding the City of Kinetics in the north. Then, her gaze moved to the jungles in the west that edged the City of Witches, grazing over the central plains housing the City of Anima—eventually landing on the Shifter crest marking the city in the south.

Her shoulders fell, mourning shadowing her gaze, dimming their metallic glitter.

"Do you miss it?" he asked, gliding up beside her to peer over her shoulder.

She remained silent for a long, drawn-out moment. When she replied, it was so quiet it was almost lost to the shelves around them.

"Every day."

The whispered melancholic words broke his heart. Kevah had wanted to see her ice melt, but sorrow wasn't what he thought he'd find beneath her glacial exterior.

He brushed the back of his fingers up her arm. "Why did you leave?"

She sighed. "It's a very long story."

Kevah leaned in close, his lips a breath from her ear. "Well, I am an excellent listener."

She turned to look at him, their lips so close that the slightest movement would have them meet—so close that he could discern every golden flake in her brown eyes.

Then she turned back to the book, smirking. "Nice try, lordling. I'd hate to bore you and have you send the library up in flames."

He chuckled as she turned the pages, lightly flipping through them. Placing his hands on the table's edge on either side of her, his chest skimmed her back. She was so close… he wanted to grab her waist and pull her even closer. Bury his nose in her hair and soak in her intoxicating scent.

When the page-turning paused, Kevah opened his eyes and froze when he saw what caught her attention. As a child, he'd studied the image for hours, trying to see himself in the man staring back at him.

A gruesome, full-page illustration showing the moments before the execution of Alvar Andelit.

Alvar kneeled, half-naked and bloody, facing the reader at the top of a grassy hill, the same one the estate sat upon. Even through the centuries, the artist captured the air of power Alvar must have held. Surrounding him were those who would become the first leaders of the new Thaumoria. The one he'd forced them to create.

Before Andelit, Thaumoria was a land with no boundaries and no rulers. The magic classes lived where they may and answered only to themselves and their neighbors. Small communities existed, but nothing like the cities of today.

Then Andelit came.

Born with the power to wield all four elements, he was the most powerful Elemental in history. He believed the Elemental Gods and Goddesses had blessed him with the power for a reason: to be the sole ruler of Thaumoria.

He'd gathered an army and stormed the lands.

His influence led to the decision that the people needed guidance, and no singular person would ever rule. So, each magic class came together and chose who would represent them.

Those representatives stood behind Alvar in the illustration.

Four Witches, the first council of Four,

held poison-tipped arrows created from the most heinous things to come out of the jungles.

The first Anima Mother, with a prey bird perched on her shoulder and a bear by her side—two of the many animals that answered her call.

The first Shifter Sage, standing proud in white robes, glowing despite their almost unidentifiable features. Stories said that no two people who looked upon them ever saw the same person.

The first Kinetic Council glared at Alvar, all stoic and harsh, with unforgiving features. Their hands at the ready, and prepared to tear him apart at the joints.

And at the center stood the first Elemental Lady, head bowed in shame for what her people had done—the only leader of the newfound Thaumoria who would not participate in Alvar's execution.

On the subsequent page was a copy of the City Establishment Treaty, signed by all the leaders pictured behind Alvar.

Atana ran her fingers over the illustration, taking in the details of each leader.

When she spoke again, her voice was no longer the penetrating attack that it had been in the garden. Rather, it was quiet and curious.

"What's it like?"

Kevah bit his cheek until the taste of blood flooded his mouth, fingers curling, gouging the wooden table until his nails bit into his palms. He didn't need to hear the end of that question; he'd heard it a thousand times.

What's it like holding so much power?

What's it like being compared to the most evil and infamous man in history?

What's it like to be the most powerful Elemental since Alvar Andelit?

What's it like?

Then she forced a breath through her nose, sounding almost amused by the idea of such a terrifying man standing so close. "You probably get that a lot."

He swallowed the biting retort he wanted to make. "You have no idea."

Kevah prepared himself for the fear. For the sudden submissiveness that always followed the realization that the world itself bowed to his will. For the fawning and groveling that came when people realized what he was capable of, what he could do for them, what he could do *to* them.

She shook her head. "It must be wonderful."

Kevah's heart stopped for a beat, then another.

He could hear the smile in her voice. Not only envy and admiration, but a yearning unencumbered by terror.

She wasn't afraid of him, of his power. It impressed her.

Kevah's own parents hadn't had the spines to deny him too much in life for fear of the legacy he followed, and the woman pressed against his chest, just a breath away from his lips, admired him for it.

They were the most arousing words he'd ever heard fall from a woman's tongue.

He swallowed hard, unable to believe his ears. "Won-wonderful?"

She glanced up at him over her shoulder. "Not that you seem to embrace it as you should, lordling." She sneered, though the ice she formed was thinner than gauze. Looking away, she studied the illustration again, her fingers running over the Shifter Sage. "I imagine it must be nice to have so much power. To have the ability to influence so many and… destroy those who have wronged you. I can't believe you pretend it isn't there."

The monster reared in his chest, the fire in his veins flaring hot. "Has someone wronged you?" The words came out low and husky, the promise of violence threaded between every syllable.

He'd known Atana for mere hours, and already, the thought of someone hurting her made him murderous. How dare someone harm the glorious, fearless woman before him? The only person, aside from Lady Aladonna, to look upon him without trepidation.

She lifted an eyebrow, the corner of her lip twisting. "Why? Are you going to avenge me, lordling?" Her chin lifted in challenge, bringing her lips so close to his he could feel her breath mingling with his. "You'd have to show off that magic of yours, and we both know that isn't your forte."

There was no hesitation at his temper. Instead, she poked at it, prodding to see what made him tick. She wanted to see that side of him. The side people hid from. The side he kept locked away, saved for training and training alone.

It was becoming clear that she saw him in the same light as those who opposed him taking the lordship: as a wavering young Elemental who showed little interest in the responsibility lain at his feet. In a way, it was true. Kevah had no interest in being the person he was fated to become and had fought against it for so long that many wondered if he deserved it.

But there was one thing no one could deny: power ruled Elementals, and power drenched every cell in Kevah's body, even if he didn't want it. Even if he fought to restrain it and pretend it wasn't there.

For the first time, he wanted to listen to

those who called him a monster when they thought he couldn't hear. He wanted to play into the reputation Andelit laid out for him, step into those shoes, and burn it all.

For the first time, the thought of seeing himself reflected in that illustration of Alvar Andelit didn't scare him. He welcomed it.

It felt… good.

Lifting a hand, he ran his fingers across her neck until his palm cupped the nape, fingers tangled in her golden waterfall waves.

"I would *burn* Thaumoria if you asked me to," he growled, a vibration rippling through the stones around them, meaning every word.

Her smirk lifted into a grin. "So dramatic."

His shoulders lifted in a gentle shrug. "What do you expect from the most powerful Elemental in generations?" The words came easier than he'd expected, which didn't bother him as much as he anticipated.

Bragging about his position and magic was drastically out of character for him. But Atana made him want to flaunt it, to scream it from the rooftops. As he boasted about what he had always tried to underplay, her gaze became hungry.

Hungry to see more, for his temper to rise. Hungry for him.

The flames around them flared, diminishing the shadows and bringing light to the library. The shadows shrank from the dancing fire responding to his lust. A growl built in his chest, rumbling beneath his feet as the very stone around them responded to the need growing within him.

Usually, he kept a tight hold on his magic, especially when he took a lover, for fear of scaring them. But with each new manifestation of his desire, Atana seemed to come to life.

Eyes widening, lips parting into something between a gasp and a sensual smile, that ice melted completely. The walls came down, if just for a moment, and he saw exactly what she desired.

Power, in every definition of the word, unbridled and wild.

And if there was one thing he offered, it was that.

"And here I thought you weren't interested in catching my eye?"

Her sassy smirk returned, filled with delight rather than aversion. "If I remember correctly, I said I had no desire to be bedded. I do not give myself to those who will forget my name in the morning. I am not a game to be won and then walked away from, lordling." She moved closer, brushing her lips against his, causing Kevah to hold his breath.

His mind swirled as he tried to think through the fog her nearness caused. He could feel her presence working its way through his mind, blurring every thought and clouding any discernible line of thinking.

"And you're still sure that by dawn…" he whispered.

"You'll think me just another mistake," she finished, moving out of his grasp.

He reeled at her absence, feeling empty in its wake. The flames flickered around them, nearly going out, as if a gust of wind had come through and tried to extinguish their light.

She gave him only moments to contain

himself and pull back the pieces she'd just torn from him. "Where to next?" Tipping her head to the side, she said the words so innocently, as if there hadn't been a burning desire blazing between them just heartbeats before. As if her round eyes hadn't just been brimming with lust.

Kevah's laugh sounded painful even to his ears. He had to force a deep breath to steady himself, running a hand over his face. When he finally moved, every ounce of concentration kept him from tripping over his own feet as he found his way to her side once again.

He offered her his arm, tensing when her fingers settled into the crook of his elbow. He wanted more, and keeping his composure was taking conscious effort.

"I have an idea," he said, leading her out of the library.

CHAPTER 6

Kevah's heart pounded as they approached a series of plain doors he was all too familiar with. He'd led them to the farthest end of the top floor of the estate, walking a path he'd taken more times in his life than he could count.

The immaculately decorated halls faded into smaller, more intimate spaces. No longer in a public part of the estate, the hallway was rather plain.

"Where in Thaumoria are you taking me, lordling?"

Kevah licked his lips, his nerves getting the better of him.

"Somewhere special."

He led them through the first door, which took them to a vast sitting room. Two large, heavily cushioned couches sat on either side of the coffee table on one side of the room. On the other was a wooden table with space enough for six to dine comfortably. More seating hugged the room's edges, making the space feel cozy despite its size.

It was excessive, if he was being honest.

Besides the women he brought to bed, guests rarely visited his rooms. Even then, he always used the door leading straight from the hallway to his bedroom, avoiding the other rooms altogether.

Atana looked around, taking in the space as he led them across the floor.

"Whose rooms are these?"

Kevah bit his lip. "They're mine. One of many."

Her head whipped around, giving him a scathing look. "What did I say about being bedded?"

Kevah raised an appeasing hand. "I know. That's not why we're here, I promise."

"Then why…"

"Because of this." He pushed open one of two double glass doors along the far wall.

Together, they stepped onto an enormous balcony that wrapped around the corner of the estate, giving sweeping views of the wealthy outlying district stretching from the estate to the edges of the city beyond. In the distance, a panorama of the City of Elementals filled the skyline. So late into the night, the city sat relatively dark, but scattered windows still glowed with light from bulbs or candles.

"It goes on forever," Atana breathed, leaning over the railing as if she'd get closer to the horizon.

"Best view in the city."

The sky was a dark, depthless sea of stars. Sunrise approached quickly, and the night was in its blackest hours before dawn.

Atana glanced over her shoulder with a wry smirk, bringing forth the woman from the gardens once again. "So, how many women have you brought out here to 'see the view'?"

A self-deprecating laugh shook Kevah's

shoulders as he leaned an elbow against the railing beside her. "None."

She raised an eyebrow at him, disbelieving.

"I swear. They may have graced my rooms, but you are the first woman to grace this balcony with me."

Atana paused, thoughtful. "Why?"

Kevah didn't know how to answer. How did he explain that the open air and freedom of the balcony felt too intimate to share with a casual one-night stand? The balcony was the only place he could release the constantly building magic he kept such a tight hold on at all hours. Suppressing it until he could embrace it away from prying eyes. Even in training, he held back for fear of hurting Lady Aladonna during practice duels. But there… so far from everyone else, he could let go.

Kevah couldn't say that, though. It invited too many questions. It revealed too much. He might be one of the most public figures in the city, but even he had secrets no one, aside from his parents and Lady Aladonna, knew.

So, instead, he deflected, turning the conversation back to Atana.

"Why did you leave the City of Shifters?" Something about the question felt important. The answer was the key to every door she kept so tightly shut.

Atana didn't spare him a glance, continuing to watch the view instead. Slowly, layer by layer, she sank back into her glacial facade. It appeared she was watching another horizon altogether. One far away. She stood there, silent, seeming to think through her answer before replying with her own deflection.

"Is it true? Has a Dark Magic child been born to the Elementals?" The questions were quiet, a whisper on the wind, but she asked them with so much conviction that they held a physical weight.

Kevah was so unprepared that he physically flinched, trying to make sense of it. Leaning a single elbow against the railing, he rubbed his palms together, unsure how to answer.

He thought back to all the hours Lady Aladonna had drilled him on giving polite political answers, but none wanted to come out for some reason. As if something was blocking them from crawling to the forefront of his mind.

"I—The—" He cleared his throat, adjusting his stance. "As of right now—"

"What did I say about lying to me?" Atana's voice hardened, her words dripping sharp icicles she could weaponize at any moment.

Kevah opened his mouth, prepared to tell her uncertainty wasn't a lie. That just because his answer was polite didn't mean it wasn't true.

Then her eyes met his, and everything inside him melted. He was a child again, shrinking beneath Aladonna's scrutiny as she questioned him about the latest trouble he'd caused.

Hanging his head, he continued to examine his hands. "We don't know. But I can assure you that if it has—"

"*They,*" she snapped. "A child is not an *it.*"

"If *they* have been born to the Elementals," he corrected, a sharp edge entering his tone, "Then *they* will be dealt with."

A breath of tension filled the space between them as she sized him up, eyes grazing him from head to toe before returning to the view.

"You're going to kill them," she stated matter-of-factly.

"Well, that is the only acceptable way of addressing the situation. I won't do it myself, but I have no doubts Lady Aladonna will give the orders."

Atana rolled her eyes before whirling on him, stepping into his space, a threatening air leaking from her.

"*Situation*," she sneered, mocking his choice of words. "A child is not an 'it,' and a birth is not a 'situation.' So many diplomatic words that mean absolutely nothing."

Despite himself, Kevah took a step back. He had no doubt he could take anyone in Thaumoria in a fight, but something about this fierce woman had him fearing for more than his physical health.

"By the Gods and Goddesses, how did we

end up here? I don't understand what this has to do with what we were discussing."

"Of course you don't understand," she spat. "How could you? How could the privileged lordling, raised in luxury with the power of the world at his fingertips, possibly understand? Understand what it's like to be born different and alone. To have those who are supposed to protect you reject you. You don't even appreciate what you have, what you were born with." Her voice rose as she ranted, becoming hoarse with emotion until she turned away, holding a hand to her mouth—like she was trying to stop the words she couldn't control.

Kevah couldn't help it. He laughed, a loud bark of disbelief echoing off the walls behind them.

"You think I don't understand what it's like to be born different?" He seethed.

Atana glared at him, ready to reply, but he cut her off before she could.

"I've been compared to the most infamous man in history my entire life. My own parents are afraid of me!"

He continued to laugh, borderline hysterical. He shouldn't be defending himself to a woman he barely knew, yet he couldn't stop. The words had built inside him for years, and since he had started, he couldn't seem to bring back his trained mask of calm neutrality.

Kevah turned to the view, throwing out his hands to embrace the city before him, which both revered and exiled him. He yelled his frustrations to the winds because they seemed to be the only ones who ever cared. "The great Lord Kevah. That's what they'll call me, right? As they cower in fear, grateful Lady Aladonna took me off their hands and raised me to be the leader I never wanted to be. I wasn't given a choice. I was *told* that someone like me has one future. One option. To become Lord."

He turned back to Atana, who continued to glare. Something like pity—or maybe it was understanding—seemed to soften her features, but Kevah wasn't done.

"Sure, I *could* say no. I could refuse to challenge Lady Aladonna for the lordship and walk away, but then what? What else is there for someone like me?

"They didn't ask me what I wanted to be when I grew up. They didn't ask me for my opinion when they came to my home at the bright age of six. My parents saw the monster their son would become and offered him on a silver platter to the only person they thought could keep him in check. You think that because I have power, I don't know what it's like to be seen as 'different' or 'other'? Think again, Shifter." Turning his back on her, Kevah felt himself deflating. Everything he'd just admitted had been a pressure in his chest he hadn't realized, and now they were out there forever—something he couldn't take back.

"I am *not* a Shifter!" Atana screamed. A broken assertion dredged up from wounds long since buried.

Breathing hard, he whirled on her. He felt like a mountain looming over the people below, staring at her small frame. He was tall and intimidating, at least that's what everyone told him, but Atana didn't flinch at his wrath.

"Then what are you?" he roared, his anger and irritation coming to a head.

They were like two predators preparing to go head-to-head in battle, a brawl between fearsome opponents whose battle cries would echo through the land… until tears rimmed her eyes, and everything in him deflated. Softening so much, he seemed to physically shrink, every ounce of fury melting away.

Whispering, he studied her, trapped by the beautiful conflict in her eyes. "Who are you?"

One would think that tears would make a woman seem small and vulnerable, but not Atana. Instead, she looked stronger and more vicious than she had the entire night. And yet, when she spoke, her words were quiet, exposing a wound she couldn't hide.

"No one you want to know," she rasped. She wrapped her arms around her, hugging herself tight, holding the pieces of herself together.

Kevah shook his head, running his fingers over her cheeks until he cupped her neck with both hands, drawing her close. "I disagree."

His nose brushed against hers, their foreheads pressed together.

"Then that's your mistake to make, lordling." She tried to make the words sound sharp, but the underlying tears only made them lonely.

It broke his heart.

Kevan, the most powerful Elemental in hundreds of years, with magic so great his existence would guarantee him a spot in history, felt… worthless. No amount of fire or water would ever allow him to fix whatever hurt the fearsome woman in his arms so thoroughly. That had made her feel like choosing her would be an act of poor judgment, her only worth embedded in her gilded beauty.

All he could do was close the space between them and kiss her. And, by some miracle, she let him.

He'd heard that the world would slow when you kissed your soulmate, that your partner became the eye of a storm, the thing that tethered you to the earth. But nothing could have been less akin to finally kissing Atana.

She wasn't the eye of the storm, calm safety at the center of the chaos; she was the storm itself.

Kevah lost himself in her, letting her whirlwind sweep him away. Every movement of her lips was the monumental force that shook the earth during a quake. Each brush of her tongue was the hurricane that destroyed ships without remorse. The taste of her was the forest fire threatening to devastate him without even blinking.

Atana didn't ground him. He didn't want her to. Rather, her clutching his jacket, pulling him closer, fueled his fire. Her gasp in the moments they parted for breath was the key to the steel collar he'd long ago clamped around the throat of his monster. His lips found her throat, desperate for more. He couldn't think, couldn't discern right from wrong as her fingers knotted in his hair and pulled him closer.

Pushing her against the wall, he didn't bother to suppress his monster. She didn't want him to, and the freedom was euphoric.

One hand braced against the wall of the

estate. Heat bloomed beneath his touch, seeping into the stone so his magic had somewhere to go. Energy crackled along his skin, and a storm built above conjured by his need. It had been years since he'd embraced his magic so thoroughly, and something about her touch, her kiss, pushed it further than he thought possible.

He could never undo whatever hurt her, but she made him want to rampage Thaumoria in her name to burn whoever it was to ash.

And when he thought he might conjure lightning out of nothing, a knock sounded at the living area door, jolting them apart and drawing him out of the moment.

They hesitated, lips panting against each other as if they hoped standing still long enough would make the intruder disappear.

It didn't, of course.

There was another round of knocking at the door, and Kevah knew he couldn't ignore it. Lady Aladonna rarely called for him at night, but he couldn't ignore it when she did.

He studied Atana's face as he pulled away,

reluctant to let her go but knowing he had no choice. Her eyes were wide as she stared at him, her lips swollen, red, and glistening.

"I need to answer that," he whispered.

She nodded slightly, looking just as bewildered as he felt.

Stepping away, he straightened his embroidered jacket, gathering himself as he did.

A hand to her lips, as if she could still feel his kiss, she turned away to face the view.

Kevah wanted to say something, anything, but he couldn't find the words.

Behind the door to his living area stood the captain of the guard, hands clasped behind his back. "Lady Aladonna wishes to speak to you," he commanded gruffly.

It was exactly what Kevah had expected. He glanced over his shoulder, back at the woman made of gold standing on his balcony. He didn't want to leave, but he had no choice.

"Is this necessary? Can't it wait until morning?" Kevah asked, desperate for an answer he knew wouldn't come.

The captain caught sight of Atana and

pressed his lips together, understanding. "Unfortunately not."

Kevah sighed through his nose, squeezing his eyes shut, and resisted the urge to let his forehead hit the doorframe. Between one heartbeat and another, he needed to become the man Lady Aladonna expected him to be. He'd let down too many walls around Atana, and he had to build them back up and face his responsibilities. When he walked out that door, he needed to be the heir Thaumoria expected him to be.

He slid that mask back into place with great effort, feeling its weight drag him down to earth and reality. "Fine, let's make this quick."

Kevah left the room, closing the door behind him.

CHAPTER 7

When Kevah opened his door again that night, his rooms were conspicuously dark and devoid of life. Hollow, empty, and quiet.

The glass doors to the balcony sat open, a salty night breeze lifting the thin curtains.

Kevah knew better than to hope, but he couldn't help but hold his breath as he stepped out onto the balcony.

The vacant balcony.

Elbows resting on the railing, hands dangling in the open air, the lord-to-be sighed.

The meeting with Lady Aladonna took longer than he'd expected. The rumors of the

Dark Magic child were getting out of hand, running wildly through the nobles, the subject of hushed conversations on every street corner.

Of course, Dark Magic children always drew attention. Only three types of Dark Magic existed, and only one of each, one Shadow Spinner, Mind Bender, and Death Bringer, ever lived at once.

Standard protocol across Thaumoria was for the parents to bring forth the child for execution as early as possible. Because of that, they could usually brush the births under the rug. Something the public didn't have to concern themselves with.

However, on the rare occasion the parents tried to hide the child until it couldn't be ignored, drawing attention throughout the city.

Even though the process was far kinder than it had been centuries prior, when people believed Dark Magic to be more prevalent than it was. They were so fearful they'd sacrifice the children and (sometimes involuntarily) sterilize the parents for fear of them bearing another.

Now, they understood that magic didn't work that way.

Magic had its own rules, randomly cursing families with the next Death Bringer or Shadow Spinner. However, just because a family bore one dark child did not mean they'd have another. The magic was so rare that the odds were almost non-existent. In modern times, so long as the parents brought the child forward, they could keep it quiet.

With the Fire Wielder couple refusing to confirm the child's magic class and causing a stir through the city, Lady Aladonna was preparing to step in.

But when Kevah sat there, listening to Aladonna discuss the proper procedure with the captain of the guard, all he could hear was Atana's words rolling over in his mind.

A child is not an "it."

The realization that they were so casually discussing the execution of an actual child made his stomach churn.

Throughout his entire life, people always

talked about those with Dark Magic as if they were inhuman. A curse, a blight, a punishment from the Gods to be dealt with. He'd never thought about them as actual… children who could play and cry and smile. Equal to an Elemental or Anima child.

They were talked about in the night, horror stories to be discussed in the dark. They were the subject of whispered nightmares spread from one child to another on playgrounds as they tried to scare their friends.

But he couldn't help but wonder what the Dark Magic child might become if allowed to… live.

It took a long time, but eventually, he'd convinced Aladonna to give it time. That it wasn't an issue they had to address immediately.

Standing alone on his balcony, Kevah wondered if it had been worth it. If spending the time fighting against Lady Aladonna had been worth losing Atana to the coming dawn.

Because as he stood there, staring out at the city in the distance, the sky lightened.

When the sun peaked over the horizon, his body sagged with exhaustion.

That morning, in the growing light of the coming dawn, Kevah went to bed alone. Just as Atana told him he would.

NIGHT AND DAY, during meetings, luncheons, and day trips to check on the Elemental ports, thoughts of Atana consumed Kevah. Her depthless golden-brown eyes, the way her kiss made him soar, the feel of his hands on her skin… he could go on and on, letting his mind wander for hours.

A snowball packed with clusters of ice smacked him in the side of the head, yanking him out of his daydreams and back into the reality that was the training room. Lady Aladonna watched him from the other end, one perfectly shaped eyebrow raised, repeatedly tossing another snowball into the air and catching it.

When she threw it, once again aiming for his head, he scattered it with a wave of his hand. Stepping through the icy spray, he thrust out a hand, sending a burst of flame in her direction, which she redirected with an air current and sent right back at him. Crossing his forearms, he shielded himself from the onslaught of flames, sending them out in all directions until they dissipated into smoke.

Kevah dug his heels into the ground, widening his stance to prepare for another attack, but Lady Aladonna only broke hers.

She glided to the refreshment station halfway between them, pressed against the far wall. Kevah met her there, recognizing the unspoken call for a break.

"You're distracted," she stated, reaching for a glass water bottle. Wrapping her hand around the base, the water chilled, creating an instant coat of condensation along the outside.

Kevah hung his head, refusing to meet her gaze as he reached for his water, not caring if it was chilled or not. "My apologies."

Lady Aladonna looked him up and down, taking in every detail. From his red hair sticking out in all directions to the new circles under his eyes, bruising his already dark skin, to how his shoulders slumped.

"Why aren't you sleeping?" Lady Aladonna had never been one for subtlety when it wasn't necessary. Her elements might have been air and water, two of the most malleable things in the world, but that didn't mean the woman who commanded them would tiptoe around things.

Kevah shrugged, not wanting to discuss his personal life with the Lady if he didn't have to.

Despite being the one to raise him, Aladonna had never been a motherly figure. When he had nightmares as a child, his mother had comforted him. Lady Aladonna taught him how to use magic to drown an enemy.

Kevah made to walk away, but an order from Lady Aladonna had him stopping in his tracks.

"Don't walk away from me."

Don't you dare lie to me.

He bit his lip, pushing Atana's voice from his thoughts, repressing the urge to argue.

With one long breath, he turned to face Aladonna again. Kevah loomed over her, even with Aladonna's significant height, yet she somehow looked down her nose at him.

She crossed her toned arms, shown off in a cropped tank top she only donned for training sessions. "What's this about? I haven't beaten you in a duel since you were fifteen, yet here you are, taking strikes to the head."

Despite over thirty years between them, Aladonna had always matched Kevah's stamina step-for-step, having never stopped training for possible duels.

Technically, any Elemental in Thaumoria had the right to challenge the current Lord or Lady for their place. Power ruled Elementals, and though they always tried to identify the most powerful among them young and raise them to be proper leaders, anyone who thought they could win in a duel had the right to do so, which meant the best Lords and Ladies never stopped training.

"It's nothing," Kevah muttered. "The time is coming when people expect me to declare my challenge, and I'm not sure I'm fully prepared to take the Lordship yet."

Lady Aladonna rolled her eyes, not buying the fake excuse. "Oh, please. I can tell one of your politically polished responses from the other side of Thaumoria, or did you forget who taught you how to craft them?"

Kevah grimaced.

"What is this actually about?"

Kevah shifted on his feet, looking anywhere but at her despite her ducking and weaving to catch his eye.

"Is this about a woman, perhaps?" she guessed.

Kevah rolled his eyes but couldn't deny it.

"I see," she drawled, a twinkle in her blue eyes. "Has a special woman finally captured our heir's heart?"

He scowled at the floor.

"At least you won't be difficult about this or anything," Lady Aladonna sneered. After a lengthy pause, during which she expected Kevah to talk, she held up her hands, giving in. "Fine, don't talk. I'll talk. You, young man, are a lord-to-be, whether you like it or not.

Pull your head out from between your knees and do something about it if you want something. Stop pretending to be common just to fit in. No woman wants a man who sits around on his ass, pretending to be something he's not."

The memory of how Atana's eyes lit up when he showed her the true depths of his magic flashed through his mind.

Before Atana, hearing Lady Aladonna tell him to embrace his status and power would have made his stomach sour. One of the banes of his life was being compared to Alvar and the fear his power brought, and he hated that he had so little choice in his fate.

But seeing Atana embrace who he was and who he would be flipped his perception of it all on its head. She hadn't been afraid of him. She wanted to see what his magic could do.

If she were there, he wouldn't have to hide.

Lady Aladonna turned away, ready to return to her rooms and prepare for the scheduled meetings.

"Do we have Lee Maccob's address on file?" he asked.

Lady Aladonna stopped, slowly turning to face him again, a satisfied smile lifting her lips.

"Speak with the captain. I'm sure he'd be happy to assist you." Then she walked away, using her Water Wielding to pull the glistening sweat from her forehead and flick it to the floor.

CHAPTER 8

If Atana wanted to see power, Kevah would show her just how powerful he could be.

The townhouse was in the middle of a residential area on the city's north side. With its deep purple door, flower box windows, and dark-washed stone walls, it was a well-maintained home on a respectable street.

Standing there, Kevah decided it was nothing compared to the Lord's estate. To what he offered.

City guards lined the sidewalk, the captain of the guard standing at attention by his side.

It was an unnecessary show of force;

Kevah didn't need the protection. Each city had a guard force to help enforce laws more than to protect their leadership, but that didn't stop them from being loyal. And Kevah wanted to show who he was and what he could command.

The band of stiff guards, standing side-by-side, hands clasped behind their backs as they faced the street, would draw attention. That's precisely what he'd wanted.

A show.

Glancing up, he thought he glimpsed something brilliant in one of the windows and felt like he was being watched. He gave the window a wild smile, hoping Atana was behind the glass.

"Shall we... knock, sir?" the captain asked.

Kevah turned his attention back to the front door.

I am not a game to be won and then walked away from lordling.

"Not today, captain."

Holding out a hand, palm up, Kevah plucked at a hint of his magic, and a ball of flame came to life in his hand. As a publicly confirmed tri-wielder, Kevah had his pick of elements—water, earth, and fire.

But flames demanded attention.

He threw out his hand, hurling the burning sphere at the purple door. Instantly, the fire caught, eating away at the wood.

Thankfully, since the building was stone, keeping the flames from destroying the house would be easy. He'd keep a corner of his mind focused on how far the destruction was going, though, to keep it from causing too much damage.

Kevah didn't want to burn down the street. He just wanted to cause a scene.

When the door burned enough for him to enter, Kevah stepped through the smoldering hole, assuring none of the flames touched him.

On the other side of the no longer existent door was a cowering Witch, sweating through his day suit.

The lord-to-be was used to seeing fear in others, but never did he think he'd revel in it. He let his inner monster surface, and when he smiled, he didn't care if it reached his eyes.

Maccob sputtered, bending as if to kneel, then straightening again. He repeated the action, turning in circles and forming half-thought-out sentences, as if his brain was resetting by the second, unsure how to respond. Kneel, bow, offer a seat, or beg for his life.

"Lord… sorry, not lord. Sir… er, heir to the… I wasn't expecting—" the Witch stuttered.

Kevah held out a hand, silencing the man.

"No worries," Kevah assured him menacingly, peering down at the quivering man. "I'm simply here to visit with the lady of the house."

"Well, well, well. If it isn't the lordling himself."

Kevah turned to find Atana halfway down the staircase, resplendent in a blush pink dressing gown, her golden hair swept into a simple but elegant twist.

Behind him, the Witch mewled at Atana's casual teasing.

Kevah only grinned.

She was as beautiful as he remembered, practically glowing in the dying firelight.

"The… Sir, Heir Lord Kevah here has come—" the Witch started.

"I've come looking for you." Kevah finished for him.

Atana slowly descended the staircase until they were face to face. She raised an eyebrow at the smoldering door.

"Was that truly necessary?" Despite the derisive words, she couldn't hide her amusement.

He stepped closer until he could take her chin in his fingers and lift her lips to his. "Don't you remember what I told you?" he whispered against them.

"You spin so many stories, I couldn't discern one from another."

His grin widened, unable to stop the shiver that ran across his skin as she continued to ridicule him without inhibitions.

"I told you I'd *burn* Thaumoria if you asked me to," he repeated.

She tutted. "I didn't ask for this."

"You didn't have to."

Kevah closed the gap between them, drawing her into a kiss that scorched him to the core.

Atana pulled away, hesitating momentarily, as if realizing why he was there. "You want me to join you at the estate."

It wasn't a question, but Kevah shook his head in response.

Whisking Atana away to the estate had been his first thought, but then he remembered how she'd shrunk in the presence of Lady Aladonna. Of all people, he understood how intimidating being in the same room as Aladonna could be, let alone living in the same building. Even if on the other side of a massive estate.

He didn't fully understand why Atana feared Aladonna and not him, but he intended to learn.

Instead, he'd made other arrangements. "No," he assured her, "I've arranged a townhouse on the edge of the city for you, should you wish to move there."

Atana gave a slight shake of her head.

"What in the name of the Gods and Goddesses makes you think this is a good idea? I have more secrets than you can imagine, lordling."

He considered her words for a moment, tempted to second guess what he was doing and what he was offering, but stopped himself.

"As do I, and if you'll allow me, I will spend every day exchanging secrets until we know them all."

Atana bit her lip, lost in thought, staring at his mouth as if remembering the feel of it on hers.

Kevah barely allowed himself to breathe as she considered, hoping it wasn't all for naught.

When her golden gaze flicked to his, he knew he had her. She was too hungry.

Hungry for power. Hungry for him.

"Captain," Kevah barked. Atana didn't flinch at the outburst, but he saw the captain jump out of the corner of his eye.

"Yes, sir?"

"Please gather Lady Atana's things."

"Yes, sir." The captain started giving

orders to the lower guards standing on the street. They filed in through the smoking remains, the door having burned down to blackened char.

He could hear Maccob stuttering half-formed protests and questions, but ignored him.

Atana smirked. "*Lady* Atana?"

Kevah shrugged again. "Has a nice ring to it, don't you think?"

She rolled her eyes, pulling away from him. "You're getting ahead of yourself."

"We'll see." He knew she was right. Kevah barely knew the woman or anything about her past. Yet, deep in his heart, he felt sure she was one of a kind—a jewel to be discovered and displayed. Cared for and kept close.

He followed her out the smoking doorway, watching her every movement as she approached the street. She didn't look out of place among the guards still there, but seemed to command their attention.

Standing by her side felt right, like finally finding his place. His purpose. His reason for embracing who he was.

He was sure their love (because there was no doubt in his mind that they would fall in love) would go down in history. When history books mentioned Lord Kevah, Lady Atana would follow close behind.

"I give it till dawn," Atana teased, weaving her arm through his.

Kevah threw back his head and laughed.

ACKNOWLEDGMENTS

Writing Dawn of a Ruinous Love was such a unique experience for me. The first third of this story came as easy as writing anything, but suddenly I hit a hard wall, and the romance felt like trying to force two dolls to kiss (if those two dolls came to life, flipped you the bird, and strode off in opposite directions). I often joked that it felt like the characters were trying to kill me out of spite because I firmly believe Kevah and Atana would refuse to show affection just to find amusement in my pain.

The main thing driving me forward, urging me to find a solution to inherently stubborn characters, was my support system. I knew that if I could pull this story off, it would be a favorite among my building community, and hearing all your words of encouragement truly kept me going.

First, as always, to my number one fan and the support that keeps my sanity from crumbling, my husband. For always picking me up, hearing me out, and helping me see light in my darkest moments.

Next, to my family. For always reminding me that even when I retreat into my mind and forget about the rest of the world they are always waiting to cheer me on. I cannot explain how much it means to me for so many to buy every book the moment it becomes available and believe in what I am trying to do.

To my beta readers turned friends. I have never been someone who has found friends and community easily, and I cannot express how grateful I am to have stumbled upon such amazing people. For showing me kindness in a lonely time, and granting me grace when plans changed. You all have truly been what I never knew I needed.

To my editor, for dealing with my continued blunders and still showing patience. I may create the world, build the characters, and design the story, but Sydney is the magic ingredient that brings it all together. Oftentimes, I get stuck, unable to see another way to write a sentence, and she goes above and beyond to make sure everything is as eloquent on paper as it is in my mind.

To my cover designers, who brought the story to life through beautiful art.

Last but certainly not least, to you, the reader. My work as an author would be meaningless without someone to read it, and I will forever be grateful for the time you've taken to give my stories a chance. For some, this is your first introduction to Thaumoria. For others, you have been a constant support, reminding me of what I'm working for. Either way, I am grateful you are here.

Forever thankful,

A.M. Eno

ABOUT THE AUTHOR

Originally from Howell, Michigan, A.M. Eno travels full-time with her husband and two cats. In 2017, she earned her Bachelor of Science from Black Hills State University, majoring in Psychology and a minor in Sociology. As a lifelong avid reader, she hopes to create worlds and characters that invite readers to fall in love and feel at home. She strives to write high fantasy series that are a safe space for people of all backgrounds.